DATE DUE

JAN 27 '95	FE 11 '97		
FEB 10 '95	AG 7 '97		
MAR 8 '95	SE 8 '97		
JY 5 '95	8 '98		
OC 3 '95	FE 19 '98		
NO 25 '95	R 6 '98		
DE 21 '95	MY 18 '98		
MR 6 '96			
AP 18 '96			
JE 5 '96	5		
JE 29 '96			
SE 3 '96			

LOVE

*

Poems by

811

Danielle Steel

DELACORTE PRESS / NEW YORK

To the man
who should have been there
when it all began,
and was at last,
   before too late,
bringing with him
   golden dreams
   and a promise long awaited
      and so worth waiting for.
To the lifetime that we share,
   the precious moments,
      cherished hours,
To the love of my life.
      To John.

Published by
Delacorte Press
1 Dag Hammarskjold Plaza
New York, N.Y. 10017

The poetry in this collection has been selected from *Love: Poems* published by
Dell Publishing Co., Inc. in 1981.
Some of the poems originally appeared in *Cosmopolitan*, *The Paraclete*, and
McCall's.

MANUFACTURED IN THE UNITED STATES OF AMERICA

Contents

✳ *1* ✳

Brand New Love

First Meeting

❋

Razzle
  dazzle
    snow scene,
my life
  so white
    so bare
      so vast,
and then
  your open
    door,
my heart
  whooshing
    toward
your arms,
  racing
    much
      too fast,
too free,
  as your eyes
waltzed
  slowly
    over me,

the cadence
  yours,
the tempo
  mine,
the music
  poured
    like
      vintage
        wine,
the magic
  of our moment
    so rare,
      so good,
        so new,
as breathlessly,
  I gazed
    at you.

Shuffled Papers

❀

Clumsily,
  but gently,
I push
  you
    from
      my head,
as I fumble
  at my desk,
shuffle
  papers,
try to see
  and think
    and do,
when all
  I find
    beneath
      my hand,
        my eye,
my heart,
  is
    you.

Your Call

❋

I wait now
    every morning,
        every day,
            for your voice,
your call
    your smile,
        your hand
            your eyes . . .
Waiting for the phone
    to ring,
I realize
    how hard
        I hope
for a reason,
    an excuse,
        a wow,
            a game,
an anything,
    a joke,
        a song,
            a ring . . .

I wait
 and then
  I hear
your voice
 at last . . .
I smile . . .
 I fly,
  I sing!

Moonlit Sunshine

✳

What
  do you
    do
for me
  with me
    to me?
You
  send
    silver
      sparkle
thunder
  moonlit
    sunshine
      shivers
through
  and through
  and through
    me.

From Opposite Ends

❋

From opposite ends
   of the earth
      we came,
trundling
   our bags,
      our treasures,
our laughter,
   our
      hearts.
From opposite ends
   of the city
      we came,
from different points
   where we
      once stood,
so near,
   yet far apart.
From opposite ends
   of the world
      we came,

silent and cautious,
  unseen.
From opposite ends
  of a lifetime
    we came,
and found
  a breath
    of magic
      hovering
        in between.
From opposite ends
  of a kiss
    we come,
to hold
  each other
    tight
      beneath
        a starry sky.
From opposite ends
  of a heart
    we smile,
two lives
  blended
    into one,
with no more
  opposites
    to approach,
but simply together,
  laughing
    and young,
the beautiful man
  that you are,
    and I.

Party Shoes

❋

Brown galoshes
  and red party shoes,
    my old life
     and my new,
my days alone,
  my life with you,
    funny funky
     old galoshes,
sad and brown and cold,
  then you, my love,
    smiling, sparkling,
     shy yet bold,
changing my life,
  my world,
    my blues,
to dazzling,
  dancing,
    party shoes

Zigzag

✻

Dashing
  zigzag
across
  the pattern
    of our life,
playing
  husband,
    mother,
      genius,
        wife,
scholar,
  chauffeur,
    student,
friend,
  then finding
you alone,
  for a fraction
of a moment,
  a sliver
    of a day,
loving
  what you are
and wish
  and try to be
in a very
  very
    special
    way.

Love's Tango

❋

In an anthill,
  in a tree,
    in a crowd
      of sixty-three,
I feel
  lost
    and then
      confused,
but smile
  at you,
    bemused,
you squeeze
  my hand,
    we swim
      for land,
you hold
  my arm
and render
  harm
    a useless thing,
      a broken
        spear.

With you,
  my love,
    I know
      no fear.
Only
  warmth
    and sunny skies
that dance
  love's
    tango
    in
      your eyes.

* 2 *

The Hurt Begins

Peeling Away

❋

I feel you
    peeling
away
    from
        me.
like sticking
    plaster
        tearing
            slowly
from a wound,
    a layer
of my skin
    soldered
        to yours
            until
suddenly
    slowly
infinitely
    painfully,
you began
    to pull,
just
    a little
        not
            a lot,

just enough
    to make me
        wonder,
and then
    suddenly
all of it
    being torn
        asunder,
my heart
    with its
        top
            popped,
drunk
    emptied,
        finished,
            gone,
                and now the
rest
    of me
        pried
            loose,
                torn free,
and I tired,
    frightened,
        crying,
            wondering
                why
you can't
    love
        me.

Only Violets

✳

Only violets,
  I only wanted
    violets,
not masses of
  red roses,
    and vulgar ribbons,
      and finery,
        and lies.
I only wanted
  violets,
just two
  or three,
    or scribbles
      in the sand,
a trinket,
  some small
    thought,
a warm hand
  in the rain,
a smile,
  an apple,
    or some trifling

      imperfection
        I could love.
Too much,
  and much too little.
A turtle,
  yes, a turtle
    would be nice too,
three-leaf clovers
  and fading leaves,
not stifling vulgarity
  and expensive emptiness.
But now I know how
  costly are the trifles,
how dear
  and almost
    unattainable.
Just violets,
  my love,
just that,
  remember it
    next year.

Silence

❋

Your silence hurts,
  it weighs heavily,
    dammit,
I cared so bloody much,
  I hurt, I gave,
    I cried,
      I wanted,
needed,
  hoped,
    the scope
      of it all
        still overwhelms me
as I paint portraits
  in the sky,
    seeing you
      in my life's eye,
      painting in
your presence
  for a thousand years
    to come,
wanting, wishing,
  hoping,
    seeing,

yet frightened
  that
    you'll
      fade away . . .
and then,
  trembling,
    I realize
      once more . . .
there was no call
  from you
    today.

No One There

*

I offer him
　silence
　　and take back
　　　despair.
I look
　for a rainbow
　　and find
　　　only dust.
I wish
　for a dream
　　and wake up
　　　in a trance.
I cling
　to a smile
　　and choke
　　　on a sob.
I tender
　my hand
　　and bring back
　　　the air.
I reach
　for the man
　　and find
　　　no one
　　　　there.

The Year of the Bears

❋

Side by side
  through the winter,
   tucked in
    like bears,
we snuggled
  and hugged
   and shared
    all our cares,
we teased
  and we talked,
and we whispered
  a lot,
until suddenly
  spring
   and at once
    you were
     not . . .
not mine
  and not there,
not here
  and nowhere,

         your eyes
             empty
                 in mine,
your lies
    never
        on time,
until finally,
    grieving,
I knew
    from your trend,
that our
    magical,
        mystical,
            marvelous
year of the bears
    had come
        to
            an
                end.

*L*ies

�֍

Where do you go
  when you go out
    for milk
      and come back
        seven hours later?
What happens
  when you park
    the car
      and go home
        somewhere else?
Whose cigarettes
  are you buying
    when you go out
    for mine
and come back
  with the wrong brand?
Whose name do you
  mutter
    in your sleep?
What heart do you
  keep
    in your pocket,
      hidden from my eyes?

What lies will you
   concoct next,
      my dear,
while I pretend
   that I don't fear
      the end
which came so long ago
   while I pretended
      not to hear
its deathlike
   footstep
      on my heart?

So go out.
   Go ahead.
Don't come home.
   Stay out.
      Get drunk.
         Get laid.
            Fly free.
I'll be here
   all night tonight,
trying to pretend
   I am
      the super splendid
         lady cool
I can't
   even
      begin
         to pretend
            to be.

Noise

❀

Motorcycle,
  airplane
    noises,
hot rock
  on the stereo
    in your car,
swift step
  and static
    always
      in the air.
Ever quicker
  pace
    hastening
      away
from peace
  toward
    noise,
playing
  volleyball
    amidst
      the people
        in your life.

Run faster
   faster
      still
midst
   your self-created
      noise
that will never
   kill
      the angry
         whispers
            of your soul.

Carved in Stone

❋

You carve me
in stone now
with your
lazy
finger
sculpting
me,
etching
the icy
nooks
you once made
soft
and warm,
you carve me
in stone
now
with the plastic
passion
of your
torch,

shooting
  tinfoil
    sparks
      at my flinching
        marble.
You carved me
  differently
    before,
turned
  my wood
    to bark,
      bearing leaves,
giving birth
  to flowers
with the powers
  of your
    burning
      love,
which secretly,
  we both know
    burns
      no
        more,
as your lukewarm,
  too weak,
    too quick
      to chill,

fraying magic
  forces me
    to speak,
when once
  silence
    was
      enough.
Now,
  after you are
    rough,
you ask
  "happy?"
    just before
      you go,
and silently
  I nod
    my head,
whispering
  softly
    "no."

Dread

❋

I dread you
  now,
dread
  your touch
and the smile
  that doesn't
    warm
      me
        anymore.
I dread you
  now,
your hand
  that frightens,
    makes me
      flinch
and hurts me
  to
    the
      core.
I dread
  you
    now,

your anger
  quicker
    than
the laughter
  that
    we
      knew.
I dread you
  now,
dread
  the sight
    of all
      that
I
  no longer
    see
      in
        you.

Peekaboo

❊

You run
    in and out
        of my simple
            life,
as though
    it were
        a game,
a child's sport,
    a sort of
        forest
where you can
    dart
        among
            the trees.
Now I see
    you,
        now I
            don't.
Perhaps you
    will,
        perhaps
            you won't.

The phone lies
   still.
It means
   you're happy
      somewhere
         else.
The phone
   then comes
      alive again.
It means
   you're tired
      of the world
         of men.
You come,
   you go,
      you flit,
         you fly.
You run into
   my arms,
you lie.
   You disappear.
And then I see
   you,
      standing there,
playing
   peekaboo

behind
a tree.
Oh, no.
No more.
This time
I score.
Farewell,
poor childish man.
Have your fun.
Live your life.
Play all your games.
But not
with me.

Cold

❋

A thousand dreams
  we shared,
    a thousand tears
    we shed,
a thousand days,
  a thousand nights,
    a thousand joys,
      a thousand fights,
a thousand episodes,
  a thousand epithets,
    a thousand hopes
      you shattered
        at my feet,
a thousand hearts
  you scattered
    and then mine,
and all the time
  I thought
    you cared,
how rare
  the joke,
    how sweet the gag,

how much I thought
    you loved
       this hag
a thousand years
    ago,
       my dear,
a thousand moments
    strung like tears,
       icicles across
          my soul,
a thousand ways
    of letting love,
       once oh so warm,
          die softly,
and then grow
    very
       very
          cold.

♪ Go

✳

I can't bear it
  anymore,
    I can't . . .
too much anger,
  too much pain,
      too much sorrow,
        too much rain,
no matter how madly
  we once
    loved
      each other,
I can't trudge
  another
    step
on this lonely
  journey
    by myself . . .
left here
  on the shelf
where you put me
  for safekeeping,
I sit here,
  always weeping,
    waiting

        for your return,
while deep inside
  I burn
     with slow despair . . .
I care . . .
  oh, darling,
     yes, I care . . .
but now I can't,
  I won't,
I will not sit here
  dying,
     fading,
        crying,
loving,
  hating,
     waiting
        for the fates
to deposit you
  in my arms
     once more
with your smile
  so rich and slow . . .
oh, no, my love,
  I can't
     love you or not,
        this time . . .
           I go.

❊ *3* ❊

Letting Go

Free

✳

Setting the bird free,
   raven haired,
      soaring high above my head,
watching him,
   wings stretched out,
with only a brief last look
   back,
circling high,
   wider now,
pride swooping low
   in my heart,
and coursing through
   my veins,
pride
   because I set him
      free,
only to remember
   all too quickly
      that it was not
        I,
      but he,
and with a last tender
   look

at my now empty
   horizon,
I know that he was
  always
    free.
Gone now,
  raven bird,
    gone to your own sun,
far from mine,
  far from here now,
much beloved bird,
  fly well,
    soar high,
      go free.

Silence on the Stair

❋

I watch
  the top
    of his head
as he travels
  quickly
    downward
into the vortex
  of the spiral
    staircase,
running
  down,
lightly
  like water
    down a mountainside,
his feet
  barely touching
    one step
before they rush
  headlong
    toward
      another . . .

he waves
  his hand,
    then looks
      up,
sunlight
  dancing
    on his face.
It is
  a moment
    filled
      with grace . . .
and then
  despair.
Before
  I gave
    my heart
      its head
to tell
  its tale,
I let him
  go,
I let him
  flee,
to dance
  his freedom
    dance
      so far from me.
Gone now.
  Gone.
And only
  silence
    on the
      stair.

Desperation

✳

In desperation
  I counted
    on my fingers
      whom to call,
to turn to,
  reach out for,
    cling to.
Seven, eight,
  nine
    people
      to hold
        close . . .
nine,
  seven,
    four,
      none.
Mistaken
  I had been
    in desperation,
finding that
  others wouldn't
    do.
I only
  wanted
    him.

Fragile Moments

❀

Shock.
  Blast.
    Zap.
      Gone.
Gone?
  Gone.
    He's gone
    now.
Dead.
  Finished.
    Over.
Yes,
  gone.
And strange
  how it
    all works,
      how it
happens,
  what lasts
    in one's
      mind.

Only the
   tiny
      fragile
         moments,
            the unlikely
gems,
   the morsels,
      and not
         the cake,
the taste
   of the whole
      forgotten,
and only
   the faint
      perfume
         of unreality
            remains . . .
his whims . . .
   his smile,
      the guileless
         way he looked
only once
   or twice,
      and in a thrice
         he's gone,

the tale
too brief
to tell,
and you remember
nothing
very long
or
very well.

Soaring Silver Bird

※

Soaring silver bird
  in the noonday
    sky,
weighted
  with the man
    who chose
      to leave me.
I wish
  for safety,
pray
  for flame,
knowing hotly,
  in the midst
    of my confusion
      that
        flame
or no
  he will be
    dead
      to me
        now.

Fear Not, Farewell

❋

Fear not,
  sweet love,
the hands
  of time,
for poems
  do not
    always
      rhyme,
fate runs
  its course
    and plays
      its tricks
and in the
  last
    and final
      mix,
one wins
  it
    all
      and loses
        naught,

if love
    was good
        and battles
            fought
to their
    very
        final
            end,
good-bye,
    sweet love,
farewell,
    my friend.

* **4** *

Alone

Princes, Toads

❋

Princes,
  toads,
    and butterflies,
sugar cookies,
  bitter apple tarts,
    and frosty lemonades,
circus tents,
  and puppy dogs,
    and hayrides,
icy midnight
  swimming
    in a lake,
muddy roads,
  woodsy smells,
    fresh grass,
and dandelions,
  and oranges,
    and wine,
faded denims,
  musty silks,
    and faded memories
of princes
  turned
    to toads.

Bereft

❉

What is it like for you right now?
  Is the snow as grayish
    as the world you left behind?
Is it all as filled
  with being busy,
is it as much effort
  to laugh harder than the crowd?
Have you told as many
  funny stories?
Have you almost cried
  as many times?
Or are you really having fun,
  the very best of times,
and feeling much relieved
  to be cavorting
    in the snow,
and very far away at last,
  feeling that you have
    escaped
before the time could come
  when people don't turn back?
Or worse,
  have you just forgotten
    everything that passed?
Are you being happy?
  Or feeling quite bereft
    the way I do?

Crash into My Life

❋

Did you mean
   to crash
      into my life
         this way,
leaving everything
   so topsy-turvy
      as you left?
Do you mean
   to tell me
      that you
         didn't know
            I'd care?
Did you really
   think I'd laugh
      and walk
         away?
How small you must have
   thought me,
if even
   for a moment
      you believed

I could
  smell roses
    in the air
and taste
  champagne
    again,
and walk
  away
    at midnight
to rake
  my leaves
    and give up
      life again.

Sketch

❄

That sketch of you
  so perfect
    at the time,
so endearing
  because you smiled
    above it
as we stared at it
  together,
    pleased.
Now it stares
  at me,
    alone,
and hangs coldly
  on my wall,
no longer part
  of you,
    or us,
no longer anyone
  I even
    once
      remotely knew.

It is but
   a strong man's
      face,
your kind
   of eyes.
A man
   in a beret.
Someone
   born here
      on my wall.
It could be
   anyone
      but you,
in fact
   it is
      no one
         at all.

Someday

❋

Someday
  is a place,
   a time,
    a dream,
a blade of summer
  grass,
    dried out,
and reminiscent
  of a day
    when someday
was reality
  and filled
   with hope.
Someday
  was a word
   we used
    to taunt
     each other,
a distant spot
  we hungered for,
   but were anxious
    not to find
     too soon.

Someday
    was a yearning,
        a man I knew
and loved,
    in a someday
        sort of way,
because today
    was never quite
        his style.
Someday
    was a child
        we would have
            had,
                but didn't,
a time I knew
    would come,
        but never has.

If I Can

How do I find my way back
 from the place
 where you
 led me?
The arbor,
 the swing,
 the lilac,
 the ring,
the promises, the dawn,
 the dreams
 that they spawned.
I understand.
 It is all different now,
 you aren't a boy,
 you're a man.
But show me, my love,
 the way back
 from it all,
and I'll follow the path
 if I can.

Boat Come In, Tide Go Out

❀

I sat and watched
  a boat
    come in,
the tide
  go out,
a bird
  fly by,
a man
  swim past,
a life
  go by.
The sun
  had set,
the man
  had gone,
the tide
  was out,
the day
  was done,
the life
  gone by
was mine.

Fingering Our Sand

❋

Going back
  to tender places,
    full of you,
touching
  once warm
    moments,
      looking at
our sun,
  standing
    twixt
      our sea
        and sky,
and fingering
  our sand,
    looking at
      the places
we both
  once wore
    like hats,

I wondered where
the moments
went,
flying past
my head
like cranes
and darting
through
my feet
like rats.

Couples

❋

Couples.
   Happy couples,
clinging close,
   hugging tight,
      dancing fast,
         being one,
laughing loud,
   singing high,
      giggling shrill,
         showing off,
loving love,
   living hard,
      and making
         my heart
break
   and
      snap
         and
die
   as
      I
         watch
         them

from
  this
    spot
      where
        I
still
  stand
    alone.

❋ 5 ❋

Trying Again:....Looking

Peacocks and Frogs

＊

Peacocks
   and frogs.
Princes
   and pickles.
Gingham
   and mustard
     and giggles
       and tickles.
Onions
   and daisies
and raindrops
   and stars.
Cheap wine
   and fine wine
     and love
       sold in jars.

Matador

❋

I play
  a matador's game
    with life,
face it
  squarely,
    deceive
      its sharp
        horns,
wave
  embroidered
    glitter
      in its face,
I flaunt
  who
    I am,
and proudly,
  in the noonday
    sun,
I dance
  for no
    audience,
save
  my own

soul,
I lust not
for blood,
merely
for life.
I stand
here
alone,
with the
cape
in my hand,
I flee
not
from battle,
I laugh
when
I can.
Ha! Toro!
See me here,
see me
now!
See me, Life!
I am
a Woman!
I am
no man's
wife.

Are You Still There?

❋

Leafing through
  the pages of my address book.
Looking for you,
  your name
    scribbled
      somewhere,
stuffed
  in my back pocket
    lo those many years
    ago.
Groping
  for you
    in the attic
      of my memory,
never
  lost,
    but put away.
Strange time
  to call perhaps,
    your name
      and face

retrieved
  so late
    after time
      has tossed us
both
  from here
    to there.
But now
  I'm here
    again.
      Are you?
Seven numbers
  and a long
    thin
      ring
        ringing on.
You must be
  gone.
    And then your voice
    again.
Surprising
  in its nowness
    right here
      in my room,
as I wonder how
  you look
    these days,

after such a lot
of years
pressed between
the pages
of a frayed
red leather book.

Pretend Forever

❀

Devastating,
  debonair,
    delightful
      man,
and I,
  the dazzling
    darling,
as face to face
  we dance,
    we waltz,
we do a minuet
  of hope
    on our desert isle,
I laugh,
  you smile,
    we float
      with glee,
Together
  hand in hand,
    so free,
then suddenly

I see
   the narrow
      band
of gold
   that holds
      you fast,
         and at last
you see
   that I am
      fettered
         by the same,
and now
   it is
      a kind of game,
         as you hold
            my arm,
I touch
   your sleeve,
      enjoying
         the pretend
            forever
magic
   of our
      cinderella
         eve.

You Too?

✿

Good-bye
  hello
    good-bye
      good-bye
hello.
  Hello
    once more.
      Yet again.
And then
  good-bye
    another
thousand
  times
  and
    more.
From
  the end
    to
      the beginning,
and then
  back
    again,

starting
  new,
    no longer
      starting
        fresh,
no
  fresh
    left.
And each
  hello
    has
      the echo
        of good-bye
hidden
  in
    its heart,
ah, yes,
  my friend,
    I know.
      Hello?
Yes.
  For a while.
    And then
      you too
        will
          go?

Twinkles and Sparkles

❀

Twinkles
　and sparkles
　　and horrible
　　　shakes,
shivers
　and giggles
　　and frivolous
　　　quakes.
Vague looks
　and dark looks,
　　odd thoughts
　　　and green eyes.
Yesterday's
　wonders.
　　Tomorrow's
　　　good-byes?

Snow in Your Hair

❋

Snow
  in your
    hair,
      not age,
warmth
  in your
    heart,
      not rage,
a smile
  in your
    eyes
      just for me,
I lean
  gently back
    and you
      are my tree.
Your heart
  has been
    farther
      than mine,

You love
    your cognac,
        your cigars,
            your white wine.
There's no
    haste
        in your
            pace,
you
    no longer
        must
            race,
no more
    do you flee
        or break
            dates,
no need
    to rush
        past,
            dodging fates.
You give me
    the sun
        and the moon
            in your palm,
you need me,
    you love me,

you make me
feel calm.
You gave me
the woman
I wanted
to be,
you hold me
so gently
and let me
feel free,
we stand
close together
and smile
at our truth.
You gave me
the sun,
now I give you
my youth.

Sacred Papers

*

Front page,
  back page,
    sports page
and financial
  section
    all a jumble? . . .
Oh, no,
  it is
    not I
      who'll make
        you mumble
in despair,
  wondering
    precisely
      where
the page one
  news
    has fled,
as you
  lie
    cozily
      abed,

sipping tea
  and smoking
while
  exasperatedly
    and in secret
      choking
wondering
  where
    in hell
      the Dow Jones
        might be . . .
Oh, no . . .
  no sacred
    rite
to be
  defiled
    by me.
Separate
  papers,
    separate
      baths,
united joys
  delighted
    laughs,
the meeting
  of two

very
   independent
      sorts,
while above us
   one big
      bright star
         cavorts
and tall trees
   which gently
      flow and bend,
and in our laps,
   two morning
      papers,
sacred
   till the
      very
         end.

For a Year, For a Day

❃

Music and singing
　and laughter
　　and bringing
daffodils
　to toss
　　in the air
and nary
　a care,
and a river
　to wear
and a sky
　to put on
　　like
　　　a cloak,
and Coke
　to drink
　　and then
　　　champagne

and carriage
  rides
    at midnight
      in the park,
and all
  a lark
    until
the gingerbread
  begins
    to crumble,
and at last
  you stand there,
    broken,
      foolish,
        humble.
Go ahead,
  sing.
    Don't wait
      for a ring.
Laugh
  while you may,
    for a year,
      for a day,
smile,
  and never look
    harried,

if the man
you insist
that you
love
is
already
married.

Only Close

❃

Yes, love,
  I know,
    it's hard
      for both of us . . .
my wanting,
  needing,
    hoping,
      waiting,
almost
  seeming
    to be baiting
as I reach
  out
    in a way
that fills
  you
    with
      fear . . .
it's
  all right,
    runner man,
it's okay,

yes
　　I know
you'll stay
　　while
　　　you can
then you'll
　　go
and I'll
　　grow,
and I'll
　　cry
　　　for a while . . .
　　　　ssshhh . . .
it's all right,
　　darling,
　　　smile.
I shan't
　　get you
　　　lost
　　　　in a life
　　　　　that you dread,
as visions
　　of wedding rings
　　　dance
　　　　in your head.
Fear not,
　　don't flee.
I only
　　want you
　　　close
　　　　to me.

Fondly

❋

I care about you.
  I like you.
I relate to you.
  I understand you.
I feel for you.
  I'm fond of you.
    You're dear.
Oh, no, my dear.
  You're not even
    here,
nor barely
  there
    with your "fond"
      words
that relate
  to like
    and care.
      You are nowhere.
I need you,
  want you,
    love you.
That's what's
  really there,
    but do you
      dare?

The Inside of Your Arm

❋

You make love to me
  as though
    you wore
      the manual
        on the inside of your arm.
You touch,
  you feel,
    you reel,
you slide
  along the inside
    of my thigh . . .
      you sigh,
you smile,
  you keep yourself aloof,
    you arch sharply
      toward the roof,
you moan,
  and then you glance
    to see if by chance

I am as transported
  as you want me
    to think you are . . .
but no,
  no different
    than the backseat of a car
      a century ago,
        and then as well
there's one tiny tender thing
  that you, m'friend,
    forgot
with all your ravishing,
  ravaging,
    macho, sexy, free! . . .
You never even kissed me.

Octopus Hectopus

✳

Octopus
  Hectopus
    Hexagon
      Round
        Lovers
who cheat
  make their own
    wailing sound,
shrieking
  like banshees
    explaining their ways,
breaking
  all hearts
    till the end
      of their days.

No Man, Our Man

Was he a man
the man
who was
my man?
You know,
that man . . .
the man . . .
my man . . .
. . . her man.
The man
who was
her man,
was mine,
I thought,
and I hear
she thought
so too.
Foolish
to think
the man
was ours.

No man,
  our man,
    her man,
       my man,
and I only
   wonder
      now and then
        who is his
woman now?

Come Back

❋

Funny
  that they all
    come back.
      They always
        do.
Back
  they come
    with a change
      of heart,
long after
  they had
    gone.
Back
  they come
    with all
      the words
        I wanted
once
  to hear.
    But they come
back
  too late.

Ears
        go deaf,
hearts
    die,
        moments
            pass
and time
    ceases
        to be
            of much
                importance.
This time
    make it
        different.
Bring him
    back
        while I
            still
                care.

Broken Day

❋

I bought
 groceries,
  forgot
   to wash
    my hair,
picked up
 a pack
  of cigarettes,
and
 eighteen
  nails,
I had
 a project,
  forgot
   a lunch,
I think
 it rained
  all
   day,
all year,
 all life
  gone
   gray.

Someone
  said
    that
      you
        got
married
  yesterday.

He Calls

❋

And now,
  at last,
    he calls,
in tears,
  in fears,
    in dread,
instead
  of having
    loved me
      then.
He calls me
  now,
    in pain,
      in grief,
        in guilt,
with endless sorrow
  for the old cruelties
    he once enjoyed
      so much.
I remember . . .
  and now
    I answer him
      with caution,

with a sigh . . .
  a distant
    something
      in my eye,
not quite a tear,
  no longer love,
    almost anger,
yet
  not
    quite
      hate,
        too late . . .
he asks
  if I will see him
    and I answer,
      cowardly,
        vague,
muttering
  "don't think I can"
    to this
pitiful,
  not quite,
    too late,
      guilty
        man.

First Hello

*

First hello
　　on a bright
　　　　spring day,
fresh green
　　splashed
　　on all
　　　　the trees,
flowers
　　everywhere,
　　　　in my hair,
our hands,
　　your voice,
a ferryboat
　　ride,
　　　　laughter,
　　　　　　songs,
and ice cream
　　cones
　　　　on a newly
　　　　　　painted
　　　　　　　bench.
Then summer
　　was ours,

we held it
tight,
grew
brown
and strong
and gay,
sailing days,
and waterfalls,
and woods,
picnics
and promises
and time
always
wanting
to stand
still.
And after
all that,
autumn
came
as a surprise,
crept up,
unfurled
its golden
hair
and scarlet
wares,

it grew chilly,
    leaves fell
        as we began
            to drift,
we had
    no picnics
        left
            to share,
barely time
    it seemed
to remember
    spring
        and salute
            our first
                hello
before
    we said
        our last
            good-bye.

On the Riverbank

❀

Two men once
  found
    me
naked
  on the riverbank
    at different
      times,
and then
  a third
    came by.
All brothers,
  all the same,
    seeking
only
  naked
    maidens
near a
  body
    of cool
      water

to quench
  their many
    thirsts.
Two men
  left me
    on that
      riverbank,
the third
  left
    me
      for dead,
and if
  a fourth
    should
      happen
        by,
he'll not
  find me
    on the
      riverbank
listening
  for his
    tread.
He'll find
  me
    armed
      and shielded,

hidden
near
a strong,
stone wall,
if a fourth
should even
happen
to find me
there
at all.

· 6 ·

...Finding...

Now I Want the Have

❊

I've faced it then,
  have I?
    I suppose I have.
The magical
  answer
    to the cannonball
      question
"what do you
  really
    want?"
I have want,
  now I want
    the have,
the touch,
  the hand,
    the real,
the feel
  of the same
    leg
cast easily

over mine
  for a decade
    of winter
        mornings . . .
for two decades . . .
  or three . . .
that same leg
  flung
    over
      me,
the same smile.
  A sameness.
Oh, God, yes,
  I'd love that.
I've tasted
  the hors
    d'oeuvres,
nibbled
  at the cakes,
    the pies,
tasted
  all the lies
    of liberty
        and free.
Who sold me
  that?

I want mine
back,
the savage sweet
of same
and same
and same again
the same sweet man
to share
a life
of love
and have and same
with me.

Hurray for the Legalized Lover

❋

Were they so wrong
the madwomen
of the fifties
who endowed
each lover
with the gift
of wedlock?
Are we so much
better off
with bedlock?
Am I so free
because
I wear no ring,
and carry only
my brave name
after all
these scars?

Ah, no,
  really,
    I think by now
I ought to
  have a medal
    or two,
a name or three
  or four
    or five.
After all
  is said
    and done
who will know
  that in fact
I was once
  very much
    in love, alive?
And with all
  our lively
    seventies games,
I begin
  to yearn
    for an endless
      fifties
        list of names.

If we're so free
  why should
    we be
      so very undercover?
Next time
  I think
    I'll find me
a name-throwing
  legalized
    lover.

Are You Comfortable?

❀

Are you
  comfortable?
Can you
  breathe?
Two pillows
  or one?
Is my arm
  crushing
    yours?
Is your
  leg
    wedged
      too tight
        under mine?
Are my hipbones
  too pointy?
    My nipples
      too
        small?
Oh, stranger

asleep
   at my side
      here
         tonight,
are you
   warm?
      Am I
         safe?
Could you
   love me
      at all?

Champagne in My Shoe

❋

Sitting here,
   with early
      morning coffee,
wondering
   where you are
   right now,
I still feel good,
   like well-polished wood,
well-oiled springs,
   waiting to see
      if the morning
      brings
you back,
   or will you wait
      till noon?
         So soon?
Or not until . . .
   tonight . . .
      and then a shaft
      of fright . . .

like sunbeams
   at my feet . . .
so sweet
   our hours
      before the dawn,
the dreams
   they spawned,
      the pains
         they stilled,
the tears they dried
   from years ago,
      oh, let it grow
all this bright
   new love
      I need so much,
your gentle touch
   like champagne
      in my shoe . . .
oh, dear new man,
   come back,
      come back,
I promise I'll be
   good
      to you. . . .

Attic

❄

Over the years,
  I have carried
boxes,
    treasures,
        objects,
            beds,
old shreds
  of people
      who had hurt
          or cared,
people I had pared
  down
      in memories
          and dreams,
people who had shrunk
  and grown,
      those who had left me
          all alone,
I carried them along,
  I sang their song,
I kept their faces
  in sacred places
      in my mind,

a kind of album of my life,
  my years as child,
    my days as wife,
      my broken toys,
        my shattered joys,
lying in myriad pieces
  near my feet,
    swept into piles
      with all the smiles
that faded all too soon,
  as I sat,
    woven into the cocoon
      you quietly unwound,
where somewhere
  deep within
    you found me
      hidden,
playing with a doll,
  a bear,
    how much I care,
how good you've been
  as I notice
    what I should have seen
      an eternity before . . .
the debris beneath the bed,
  the brittle chaos in my head,
    the wilted flowers,

            forgotten hours,
the whispers and the taste
    of ash
        buried in the attic
            of ~~my not~~ so many years,
and suddenly the tears
    seem to have mattered not at all,
it is no longer fall
    but spring
        as you bring
            me all this joy
                to have and hold
                    and keep,
and I,
    laughing,
        pull aside the blinds,
let in the sun,
    hitch up my skirts,
        pick up the broom,
and finally,
    begin
        to sweep.

Brand-new Now

❋

Let us not
  confuse
    the actors
      in the play.
He hurt me,
  she broke
    your heart.
He left me,
  and she was
    a rotten cheat.
Let us instead
  see only
    each other.
You took
  my pencil,
I failed
  to wash
    the tub out,
      dry your razor,
we forgot
  to buy

a loaf of bread
for lunch.
Those are
our only
griefs
to cry for.
So if he
left me
long before
you came along,
I bid him now
adieu,
and if she left
you broken,
I'll help you
to begin anew.
And tomorrow
you'll give
back
my pencil,
I'll dry
your razor,
wash the tub out,
and we will buy
the bread
together,

and start
a solid
you-me-now
life.
Only me
and you.

• 7 •

...Loving...At Last!

Cool

❉

Okay,
  okay
    so
      I'll be
       cool.
At least
  I can
    pretend
     to be,
since
  you can't
    see
      me
near
  the phone,
    or lying
      in the bath
       at night,
wondering
  if
    you'll
      marry
       me.

Too Much

✳

Silence today . . .
  too busy?
    You couldn't
      get through?
What does it mean?
  Are you already bored?
    Does it matter?
      Is the telephone
        out of order?
I check my watch
  again
    and fiddle with
      the border
        on the bed,
running reasons
  through my head,
    thinking
      of all the possibilities,
why perhaps you
  couldn't call
    last night . . .

but still
  a chill
    of fright. . . .
        Does it matter?
        Has he fled?
And slowly,
  I go back
    to bed,
heavy hearted,
  lonely,
    and a little bit afraid . . .
Have I played it wrong
  this time?
Too open?
  Too much too soon?
    Or is it something
      that I've said?
Or have I quickly become
  just anyone,
a someone to take
  for granted,
    an old shoe?
Or is it that I am
  already
    much too much
      in love
        with you?

Nary a Care

※

You're gone,
  new lover.
Gone
  to your day,
    to your life,
      to your way
        of doing things,
whatever it is
  you do,
    when you are far
      from me.
And I,
  like a child
    with a dream,
gaze
  starry-eyed
    into the summer
      rain,
feeling anguish,
  gentle
    pain,
fearing
  you will vanish

from the bright
universe
    we created
        side by side
            last night.
And then,
    in bittersweet
        despair,
I linger
    with a cup of tea,
        fearing
you have forgotten me,
    feeling foolish,
        old with fright,
            yet young
                with promise
long forgotten
    in my distant
        dreams. . . .
And suddenly,
    you're at
        the door,
full of brand-new
    schemes
        for this path
            we choose
                to share.

Home from your wars,
   from your tasks,
      from your day,
         with nary a care
and only more love
   to strew
      on my way.
I rush
   to your arms
with a gurgle
   of laughter,
      a thunder
         of glee.
Dream man
   come true,
you actually
   did
      come back
         to me!

Sunshine Dancing

❋

Heavenly, heavenly
  mornings
    unraveling
      our bodies
and then tying them
  in a fresh knot
    with sleepy smiles
    and tender words,
as morning birds
  sing past our window,
    sunshine dancing
    on our life,
and I for the first time
  ever
    feeling like
    a wife,
yet lover, friend,
  making breakfast,
    smiling to myself
as I burn the toast,
  and break the eggs,

still feeling
   your hands
      and kisses
         on my legs . . .
surely this is what
   life
      always had in store . . .
oh, darling,
   you make me ache for you,
      always hungry,
         always glad,
            always wanting more . . .

Friend

✻

My house
  my car
    my bed
      my arms
my life
  my soul
    my smiles
      and all
        my dreams
are touched
  by the magic
    of your
      sounds,
your
  smell,
the perfume
  of your life
intertwined
  with mine
    in a silvery
      blend,
so that I can

think
of only
you,
precious
lover,
partner,
friend.

Comfortable

❁

You shout at me
  and I yell
    back,
you push,
  I shove,
and we squabble
  comfortably
over who sleeps
  where,
which side,
  whose spot,
you are,
  I'm not,
you won't,
  I will,
you grouse,
  I'm shrill,
a symphony
  of loving,
a song
  for every day,
a way

to say
   "I love you"
      in our own
         familiar way.

Matching the Pairs

❋

The roof
  brought down
    around
      our ears,
the curtains
  wrapped
    around our
      heads,
all our apples
  so carefully
    stacked,
so instantly
  scattered,
    the patter
      of every day
halted
  as we sat there
suddenly
  lame,
suddenly tamed
  by life

and anger,
fear,
and despair,
dismay,
as we glared
from
opposite
corners,
throwing rocks
tossing dreams
like used socks
somewhere
behind us
into a place
we would never
find
again,
and then scurrying
about,
clutching
our accusations
in our arms,
the charms of each
forgotten
until the magic
clock
began to chime

the hour . . .
    not quite midnight
        yet,
still time,
    a moment or two,
        in which to run
and dash and hurry,
    scurry about
        again,
            finding the socks,
                washing them clean,
asking each other
    "what did you mean,"
        matching the pairs,
            saying "I care,"
and just enough
    time
        to run
            from doom,
and meet once again,
    in the heart
        of the room,
holding out hope,
    baring our souls,
feeling my insides
    no longer cold,
        but slowly warm,

slowly glad,
  slowly good,
    slowly new,
and you with that
  smile,
    the same
      much loved
      you.

Each of Us

※

Each of us
  with our
    secret gifts,
magic potions,
  lovely notions,
    waiting to be
      shared,
waiting to be
  aired,
each of us
  a half,
a whole,
  a mind,
    a soul,
      a heart,
and yet
  a part
of a better
  richer
    more,
      looking for the
door,
  the key,

The Gift of Love

❋

Ever hopeful,
    filled with dreams,
        bright new,
            brand-new,
                hopeful schemes,
pastel shades
    and Wedgwood skies,
        first light
            of loving
                in your eyes,
soon to dim
    and then you flee,
        leaving me
            alone
                with me,
the things I fear,
    the things you said
        burning rivers
            in my head,
bereft of all
    we shared,

my soul
　　so old,
　　　so young,
　　　　so bare,
afraid of you,
　　of me,
　　　of life,
　　　　of men . . .
until
　　the bright new
　　　dreams
　　　　begin again.
The landscape never
　　quite the same,
　　　eventually
　　　　a different game,
aware at last
　　of what I know,
　　　and think,
　　　　and am,
　　　　　and feel,
the gift of love
　　at
　　　long
　　　　last
　　　　　real.